Some more titles in the

CARTWHEELS

King of the Castle

Mary Hoffman

Illustrated by
Alan Marks

Hamish Hamilton
London

For Joss

HAMISH HAMILTON CHILDREN'S BOOKS

Published by the Penguin Group
27 Wrights Lane, London W8 5TZ, England
Viking Penguin Inc., 40 West 23rd Street, New York, New York 10010, U.S.A.
Penguin Books Australia Ltd, Ringwood, Victoria, Australia
Penguin Books Canada Ltd, 2801 John Street, Markham, Ontario, Canada L3R 1B4
Penguin Books (N.Z.) Ltd, 182-190 Wairau Road, Auckland 10, New Zealand
Penguin Books Ltd, Registered Offices: Harmondsworth, Middlesex, England

First published in Great Britain 1986 by
Hamish Hamilton Children's Books

Copyright © 1986 by Mary Hoffman
Illustrations copyright © 1986 by Alan Marks

Reprinted 1987

British Library Cataloguing in Publication Data

Hoffman, Mary
King of the castle.—Cartwheels
I. Title II. Marks, Alan III. Series
823'.914[J] PZ7

ISBN 0-241-11891-3

Printed in Great Britain by
Cambus Litho Ltd, East Kilbride

It was the best sandcastle Joss had ever made.

He had built it high on the beach so the sea wouldn't wash it away.

Now his mum and dad were calling him and he could see they were the last family left on the beach.

"Good," said Joss. "Everyone has gone. Perhaps my castle will still be here in the morning."

Joss and his mum and dad were staying in a little house near the seaside. Joss looked out of the window. It was getting dark. He thought about his castle.

"Please let it still be there," he wished.

And it was. The next morning Joss and his mum and dad went down to the beach. They were the first family there.

"First on and last off," said Mum.

Joss found his castle easily. It hadn't crumbled or been trodden on by dogs. But something was different. He bent down and looked through the windows.

He could hear the sound of a trumpet.
Suddenly he saw who was blowing it.

It was a little herald with his eyes wide
open in fright.

"What are you doing in my castle?" asked Joss.

"It's not yours," said the herald. "It belongs to the Sand King."

"But I made it myself," said Joss.

"Have you come to see His Majesty?" the herald went on.

"Er, yes, all right," said Joss.

"What is your name?"

"Joss Allen," said Joss.

"Jossallen the Giant to see His Majesty," called the herald and disappeared.

The King came to the top of the flagtower. He bowed to Joss.

"Thank you for building me such a splendid castle. I have been waiting a long time for one," he said.

"But, Your Majesty," said Joss, "there are lots of castles on the beach. Why did you choose mine?"

"A Sand King can only take a Giant's castle if it lasts overnight. Most of them are washed away by the sea," he said sadly.

"Who else lives here?" asked Joss.

"Just the queen, the prince and princess and the army," said the Sand King.

The King pointed down into the courtyard where Joss could see the little soldiers marching in pairs.

Suddenly Joss heard a girl's voice.
"Did you make that castle?" she asked.
Joss nodded.
"My name's Jamila," said the girl.
"Mine's Joss. Can you swim?"
"No, I don't like the water," said
Jamila. "I like making castles. Yours is
really good."

Suddenly she jumped and said "Oh!"

"What's the matter?" asked Joss.

"There's a *person* inside the castle," whispered Jamila.

Joss decided to explain everything. Jamila seemed the sort of person you could trust to keep a secret.

Every day Joss and Jamila went to the beach and talked to the King in his castle.

One day it was too rainy to go to the beach. Mum and dad took Joss to a museum instead.

After that they had fish and chips in a café. Joss would have enjoyed it but he kept thinking about the Sand King.

Would all the rain spoil the castle?

But the rain stopped in the afternoon and in the evening there was a beach party. The children were pleased to see that the castle was still there.

"What's that?" said Jamila, pointing at the castle.

Joss saw lights and could hear faint cries.

The children slipped away from the party. As they got near the castle, they could see there was a battle.

The Sand King was leading his army out of the castle gate.

The castle was being attacked by another army from the sea. They looked very fierce.

Joss and Jamila were quite scared but they went closer. When the attackers saw them they screamed and started to run back into the sea.

"The Giants are coming!" they cried.

Joss and Jamila looked surprised.

The Sand King smiled at them.

"Thank you, my friends. You saved us
from a terrible battle."

"Who were they?" asked Joss.

"Invaders from the sea," said the King.
"They wanted this castle. But you scared
them away. You must come to our
celebration Ball tomorrow night."

"But how will we get in?" asked Jamila.

"Wait and see," said the King.

The next evening Jamila and Joss went to the beach. It was just getting dark.

They saw coloured lights shining from the windows of the castle.

When they got to the flagtower, the little herald was waiting for them.

"Welcome to the Ball!" he cried. "You must come and lead the dancing."

"But how?" asked Joss. "We're too big to get inside the castle."

"You must wish upon a star-fish," said the herald. "I'll help you.

Half a star
Half a fish,
Give the children
What they wish.

Now — close your eyes and wish!"

Joss and Jamila did as they were told and when they opened their eyes they were on the top step of a huge golden castle.

Carriages were arriving at the gate pulled by sea-horses.

The herald came to welcome them in.
He was taller than them now.

"Come on," he said. "The King and
Queen are waiting."

It was the best party that Joss and Jamila had ever been to. The King started the Ball by dancing with Jamila and the Queen danced with Joss. They danced till their legs ached. Then they ate a huge feast and listened to the music.

When the last candle had burnt out and
the day was getting light, the children
found themselves back outside the castle.
They were their normal size again.

The next day was the last one of Joss's holiday. Jamila was going home too.

They went to the beach for the last time.

"It's gone!" they cried.

The sand had been washed smooth by the tide. At first they thought there was no trace of the castle left. Then Joss found a tiny glass bottle.

Inside was a very small piece of paper wrapped up tight. They pulled out the stopper and gently unrolled the note. It said:

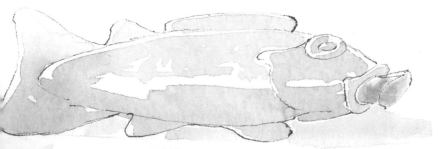

Goodbye, Joss and Jamila.

I have gone to my winter castle under the sea. Thank you for saving us from invaders. Please make me another castle next summer.

Your friend,
The Sand King.

Joss gave Jamila the bottle, but he kept the note — to remind himself to come back next summer.